D1360716

THIS CANDLEWICK BOOK BELONGS TO:

_____

_____

_____

_____

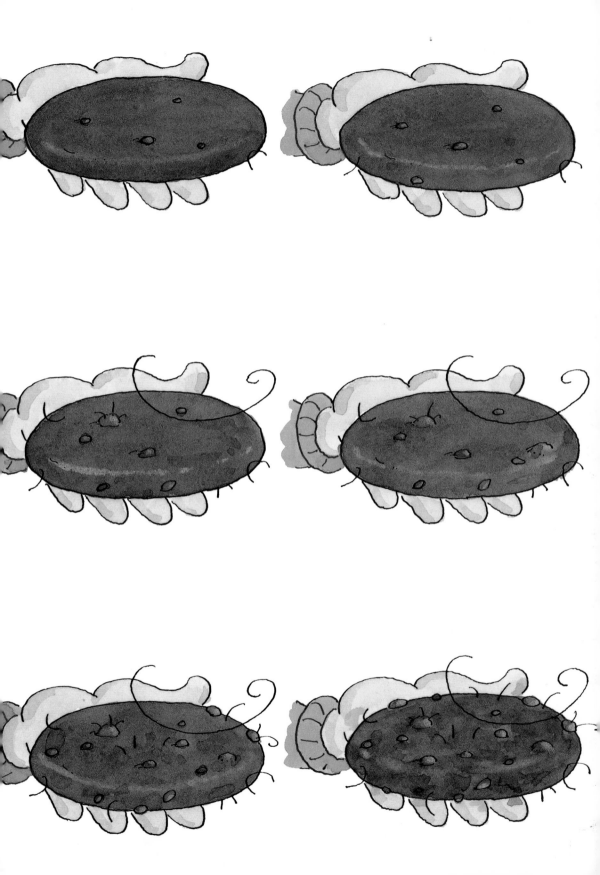

To Michael and Patrick,
who have to fight their mother
for the last chocolate cookie . . .
J. R.

To Matthew

jqR
Rix, Jamie.
The last chocolate cookie

First U.S. edition 1998

Library of Congress Cataloging-in-Publication Data

Rix, Jamie.
The last chocolate cookie / Jamie Rix ; illustrated by Arthur Robins.—1st U.S. ed.
p   cm.
Summary: When Maurice takes the last chocolate cookie at the table,
and his mother tells him to offer it to everyone else first, he travels around
the world and into space to fulfill that requirement.
ISBN 0-7636-0411-9
[1. Sharing—Fiction. 2. Cookies—Fiction.] I. Robins, Arthur, ill. II. Title.
PZ7.R5255Las   1997
[E]—dc21   97-7303

2 4 6 8 10 9 7 5 3 1

Printed in Hong Kong

This book was typeset in Beniolo.
The pictures were done in watercolor and ink.

Candlewick Press
2067 Massachusetts Avenue
Cambridge, Massachusetts 02140

THE LAST
CHOCOLATE
COOKIE

Jamie Rix

illustrated by
Arthur Robins

CANDLEWICK PRESS
CAMBRIDGE, MASSACHUSETTS

There was one chocolate cookie left
and it was shouting, "Maurice, eat me!"
So I leaned across the table
and did as I was told.

"Maurice!" gasped my mother.
"Where are your manners?
Offer it to everyone else first."
"*Everyone* else?" I said.
"*Everyone* else," she insisted.

So I carried the last chocolate cookie
around in my pocket for the next six
weeks and did as I was told.
I offered it to . . .

my brother,   my father,

my grandma,

and the cat . . . but they didn't want it.

I offered it to . . .

the papergirl,

the mailman,

my teacher,

and a lunch lady . . .

but they didn't want it.

I took a train to the city and offered it to . . .

a window cleaner,

a bus driver,

a businessman,

and a stone lion . . .

but they didn't want it!

I flew around the world and offered it to presidents and kings . . .

So I took the last chocolate cookie into space and offered it to a space monster. But the space monster didn't want the chocolate cookie . . .

he wanted me!

"Maurice Monster!" gasped his monster
mother. "Where are your manners?
Offer the human being to
everyone else first."

"*Everyone else?*" he said.
"*Everyone else,*" she insisted.

So he carried me around in his pocket for the next six weeks and did as he was told. He offered me to . . .

his brottleswat,

his fatter,

his gramench,

and the cattapurch . . . but they didn't want me.

He offered me to . . .

the pamplemoy,   the sackforth,

the dillyco, and his cybernetic expositor . . .

but they didn't want me.

He took a shuttle to **Mars** and offered me to . . .

a mickleman,   a stork rauncher,

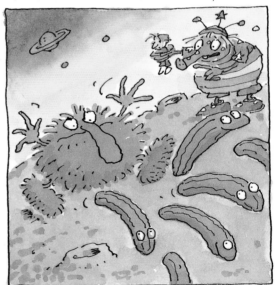

a petrified gork, and a cumber catcher . . .

but they didn't want me!

He flew around the universe offering
me to Startling Commanders
and Hairy Wingos . . .

but they didn't want me.

So he took me back to Earth and
offered me to my mother.
"It's nice to see a space monster
with such lovely manners," she said.
"I'd be pleased to have him."

I told my mother that I'd offered the
last chocolate cookie to everyone else,
but nobody had wanted it.
"Then you can eat it," she said. "It will
taste twice as delicious now that you've
been so polite."

I was dribbling. I'd waited a long time
to eat the last chocolate cookie.

I took a bite . . .

it tasted like cardboard gunk-gloop with hairs on it!

Do *you* want the last chocolate cookie?

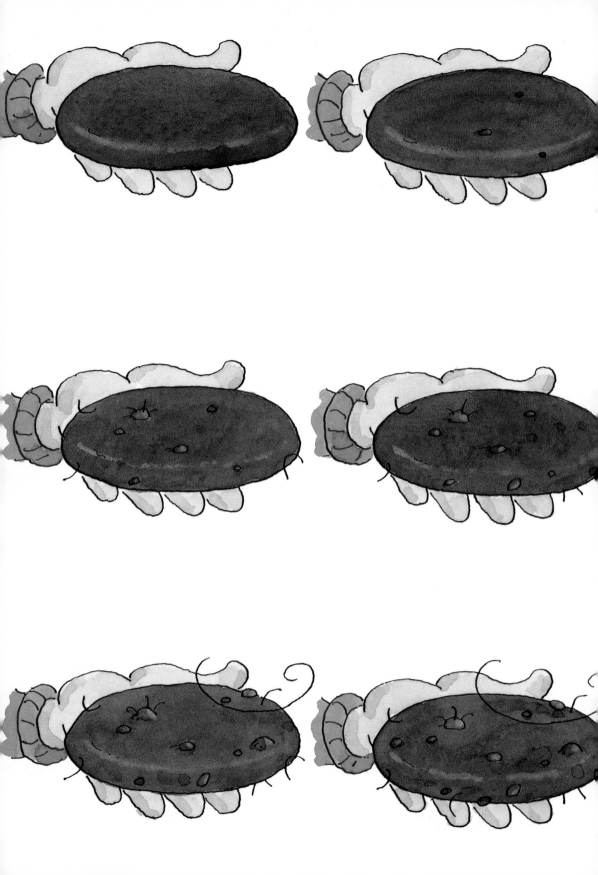

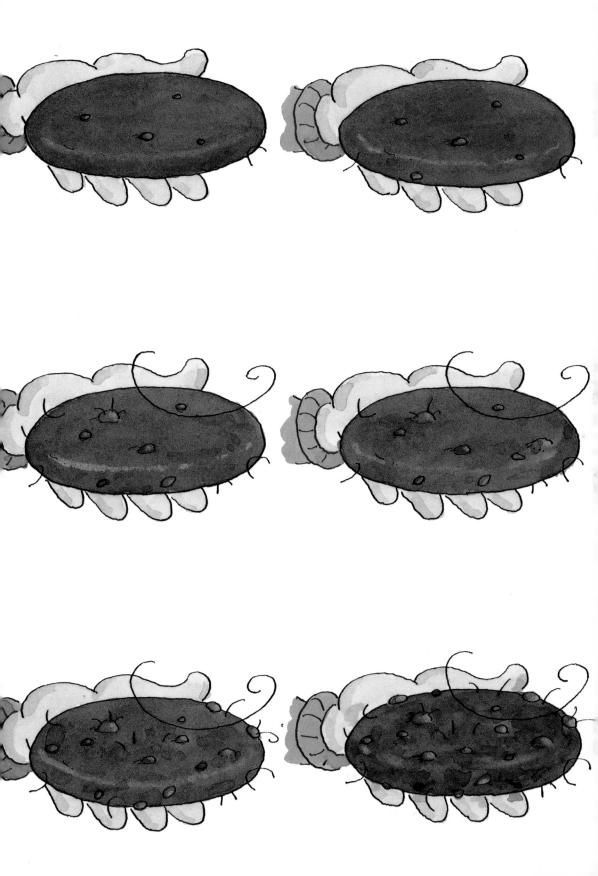

Jamie Rix is a producer and director of comedy television and radio shows, as well as an award-winning author of stories for children. He says that sibling rivalry launched his writing career. "My younger brother and I competed to see who could tell our children the scariest bedtime story. And then we bet who could write down his story first. Now my brother also spends most of his time writing novels and stories."

Arthur Robins began his career in advertising as a free-lance artist and designer. He has since become the illustrator of numerous books for children, including *What Use Is a Moose?* by Martin Waddell, *Knee-High Norman* by Laurence Anholt, and the series *Where Did I Come From?* and *What's Happening to Me?* by Peter Mayle.